Beautiful Blues

Farzana Habib

Ukiyoto Publishing

All global publishing rights are held by

Ukiyoto Publishing

Published in 2022

Content Copyright © Farzana Habib

ISBN 9789362695956

All rights reserved.
No part of this publication may be reproduced,
transmitted, or stored in a retrieval system, in any
form by any means, electronic, mechanical,
photocopying, recording or otherwise, without the
prior permission of the publisher.

The moral rights of the author have been asserted.

This is a work of fiction. Names, characters, businesses,
places, events, locales, and incidents are either the
products of the author's imagination or used in a
fictitious manner. Any resemblance to actual persons,
living or dead, or actual events is purely coincidental.

This book is sold subject to the condition that it shall
not by way of trade or otherwise, be lent, resold, hired
out or otherwise circulated, without the publisher's
prior consent, in any form of binding or cover other
than that in which it is published.

This book of poems is dedicated to Sam

Contents

Still	2
One step closer	3
Not there and not on purpose	4
The Finish Line	6
Feeling Light	8
Note to self	9
Wasted	10
Come Back	12
My Heart	13
Bad at Love	14
My Sincerest Apologies	15
For Peace	17
Abnormal	18
Missing You	19
Torment	20
Realization	21
Smoke	22
On Paper	23
The Hurtful Truth	24
What hurts the most	26
The Answer	27
Like a spirit	29

Words	30
Happiness	33
Like A flower	34
In love with the dead	35
Time Apart	36
Heartache	37
Just my 2 cents	38
Going out tonight	40
Not the Right One	41
Some Things Never Change	43
Normalcy	45
Years Later	46
Ice cream Sundae	48
365	49
About the Author	*52*

POEMS

Still

Cool weather
Quiet atmosphere
Soft glow
Calm thoughts
No aggression
No anxiety
No panic
Zen like state
Never thought I would get there
But now that I'm here
I don't want to leave

One step closer

Classes are finally over
I won't hear the bell anymore
I can put away my books
at least for awhile.
Hide my book bag under the bed
throw my library card, and student Ids into a memory
box
as I wait for the final results
pass or fail?
my heart says I will pass this time
bring home the piece of paper my eyes been longing
to see for so long
a expensive piece of paper I wish to cherish for just a
moment
show mom and tell dad
My college diploma

Not there and not on purpose

I have always been this way
never got tested for it
always called out for it
ever so often thought about it
on the days I feel extremely frustrated at
myself
You tell me something repeatedly
to do something
to not do something
pay attention to this detail or that one
be more mindful
I wonder what that even means
I always promise that it won't happen again
I will do better next time
vow to go without it forever
I can do well on my own for a while
a short period of time
then I go back to square one
in a room
the lights burning my skin
heartbeat elevated
your screaming in my face
shaking your head in disapproval
throwing your hands in the air
storming out of the room
speeding out of here in your car
slamming the door shut
just to get away from me
forget what my face looks like for a while

it always ends the same way
I do nothing anymore
don't protest
a sad smile forms
I walk away
I sometimes feel dejected
sad and tired
so tired of it all
tired of you
like the worst subject in school
like a dead end job with no future prospects
like an addict's highs and lows
I will admit that when I am like this
I am walking away from you
towards the train station
where the train of my thoughts leaves
frequently now
I don't know why this happens
I don't do it to spite you
I don't do it on purpose
Am I looking for a break?
An inner escape
a way to transport myself to the rare moments
of my life
that were blissful happy and care free
every time you start speaking?
I just don't know
so I will leave this words behind
like a farewell letter
for someone else to decipher
I promise I don't do it on purpose

The Finish Line

I think I will be able to make it this year
It's within my reach now
Part of my vision
It took a long time to get here
I gained friends
Lost many along the way
Succumbed to personal wars
Spiraling hopelessness
Inner demons
Guilty pleasures
Sweet nothings
Have the scars and marks to prove it
The sleepless nights
The lonely evenings
Endless tears and frustration
Nearly choked my inner strength
Own voice
Sweet soft innocence fleeting
Cold hard reality finally setting in
I'm ok with that
I know my own worth now
Not going to forget it
Not going to settle for less

Not going to be pushed around anymore after this
I will take all that's mine
Imagine the very best outcome
Prepare to get it and then some
No longer afraid of standing on my own

Feeling Light

There is rainfall everywhere
but the sun shone in my mind the entire time
my stormy sadness went away
a rare spring in my steps
what was left behind was a trail of flowers
all the way home

Note to self

There is loneliness
because of you
Sadness and grief
because of you
I have cracks
because of you
There are tears
because of you
There is pain
because of you
There is silent suffering
because of you
But I smile
Refuse to break
Crumble
Lose
Wither away
because of you

Wasted

the night has began
everyone is asleep
or preparing for sleep
my demons are wide awake
their eyes glisten through my very own
their hands and feet wait in anticipation to do
something wild
reckless and crazy
go on out with spiky heels on
wear a flask of gold
carry one more for a very good time
perched on the hood of some man's car
no name
no number
slithering fingers
wet lips
heavy breathing
complete darkness
awake again
disheveled hair
ripped shorts
whiskey shots
chocolate sauce
bubble gum lip gloss
quick thrusts
cigarette breath
no goodbye

sated
looking for the keys to the front door

Come Back

What should I write about tonight?
right this minute
as he snores softly in the next room
the rain fall down
comforting like a favorite song
the lights continue to glow
sometimes they flicker like a dying wish
my skin is warm from his tainted fingers
my lips yearn for more of those hot rummy kisses
my head is spinning but just slightly
images of you
of your face
body
embrace
so far away from it all
I pull the thin cover around my shoulders just a little more
suddenly aware of my nakedness
I want to get up but I can't
he says I am beautiful
but I don't want to see what he has done to my face
I want to run away from here
but I can't
not until you come back
not until your debts are all paid off

My Heart

It's in a metal cage
Locked up tight
A dozen chains
The key is lost
under the sea
I think
Many have looked for it
Only to later give up
As for myself
I don't ever want it to be found
Let it erode away like old feelings
Crusty and unrecognizable
rusty and wrapped in seaweed

Bad at Love

It's taking all that I have right now, to not reach for the phone
Call you up
Even though we fought last night
And you said you didn't want to ever hear my voice again
I admit it
I don't have any control
I forget about self respect
Anger dissipates
I'm left to drown in my own sorrow.
when it comes to you every single time
I don't know why I need to be so close to you
Even though we're miles apart
After all that, you put me through
I don't know why I need you so much
Even after you beat my heart black and blue
Every sigh that I take is a bloody one
Lots of you just translate into an ache I have no explanation for
All those broken promises license to my brain
Our unhappy ending Leaves me gasping at night
Wishing that things had been different
I still wake up with a familiar stabbing pain in my chest.
That's when I know I am missing you the most

My Sincerest Apologies

Love hurts so bad but feels so good
I didn't know that until I set my eyes on you.
I knew I fell hard for you.
Eyes open.
Emotions running wild.
Common sense out of the freaking window.
Call it fate.
Call it destiny.
Or maybe just stupidity.
Didn't know what, I was getting into.
Maybe this never should have happened.
You taught me love.
Showed me that it exists.
Let me know that it hurts like a bitch too
Told me that the scars would stay.
You were someone that saw the good in me.
You saw all the things I could not see.
Insecurities were compliments.
Complaints turn into flirting.
Flaws almost nonexistent.
But still I fell short somewhere.
I tried and tried.
Some days it was not enough.
Never enough to make you really happy.

Sorry about all the problems.
I tried some more.
Sorry about the heart break and the pain.
The broken promises and wasted energy.
I broke you down.
I know it.
I didn't mean it.
I can't make you whole again.
Not ever.
I can see the cracks all the way from here.
Is the glue supposed to be the love that I still have for you?
I still love you.
I will always love you.
But I suppose it's best if I do it from a distance.

For Peace

I wish I could rip my own heart out
throw it on the floor
and walk away from it
forever

I wish I could break open
the small part of my mind
where all my feelings for you lies
smash each feeling
one by one
till there is no love left

I wish I could pour all the love I gave to you
into something else
I will never be whole again

Abnormal

You were a lot of things
smart, funny, beautiful
but mostly chaotic
I pleaded for peace and forgiveness
It never came
What I didn't know was that I had become addicted
to chaos
Anything bland, boring and dull
got under my skin
Comfortable silence disturbed me
Normal behavior
kind words
loving gestures
put me in a frenzy of emotions
I don't understand it
I didn't know how to explain it
I continue to wait for the shoe to drop
for the monster to make his appearance again
I know I am not safe
but this is all I know

Missing You

I will wait for the day you come to the phone
I will count the minutes till I can hear your voice
again
I miss you so much
this is scary to admit because I thought I had
forgotten how
I am saddened to know that you suddenly felt the
need to pull away from me
Leave me completely alone again
broken
shattered to a degree
somehow still breathing
Even though it really hurts to breath

Torment

I wait by the phone
I wait online
I wait by the mailbox
Hoping that you will call
Hoping that you will show
Hoping that you will write
To tell me that you miss me
To let me know that you still think of me
To remind me that you still love me
The day starts off with hope
The day ends up with disappointment
Yet I continue to do this to myself
inflict pain
accept punishment
All because I can't seem to stop thinking of you
Knowing all too well that I will never forget you
nor love somebody as much I have loved you

Realization

Maybe It's just me
I'm broken
jaded and nothing phases me
but too broken to love
can't love you the way you want to be loved
I still feel something
sometimes there is numbness too
but I care
I know I do
Maybe I can't recognize love anymore

Smoke

You knew where your faults lay I didn't
You knew what you lacked but I didn't
You knew where you went wrong, I didn't
you know that you could not love me
in the way I needed to be loved
but you tried anyway for my sake
no sorry you pretended to for my sake
I wish you hadn't done that
It left me confused and frustrated
every single day
every time I see you
I wish you had been honest with me from the start
with time
my problems became minor
my emotions were dismissed
my concerns were all made up
you say you love me now
but I don't believe it
how can you give up and move away so fast
when you are in love with someone

On Paper

I love you with each breath that I take
I love you with each tear that falls
I love you with prayer that I make
But when the time comes to talk, I can't
I can't tell you all the things that I want
I can't tell you just exactly how much
I love and miss you
Because I have worked so hard to not fall apart
to always stay composed
to make sure that you don't see me in pieces
We laugh
We joke
We talk as though we had never parted ways
We laugh like nothing had ever gone wrong
Even though we are now oceans apart
I still cannot tell you how much I love you to this day
explain it to you in a way that makes sense
I don't know what to expect
I don't want to fall again
This time I know that I don't have the strength
This time I know that I don't have the patience
This time I know that I don't have the power
to put back the fallen, broken and misshapen pieces
back together again

The Hurtful Truth

You taught me about love
You told me to let it in
you showed me all the different colors
you brought them along
you forget to warn me about the pain
or maybe you did not think it was important to let me
know at all
Pain
so much of it
It stole away all the color now
one shade at a time
Everything is in black and white
sometimes grey and hazy when I am confused
Red when I don't know where to go or what to do
when I remember you
I don't know how much I am suppose to take in
how much of it I am supposed to suppress
Something has changed
Numbness
pain from you
from her
from him
It steals another piece of my heart
it clouds my mind

leaves me numb for days
I don't like who I have become
I can't look in the mirror anymore
what choice do I have
Its heartbreak now
then death later

What hurts the most

The first few seconds
When you get up in the morning
You hold a precious picture of him in your mind's eye
Only to open your real eyes to see that it's all gone

The Answer

Do you love me he asked me
I had to pause
even though I knew the answer to that question
Liquid courage was a lovely shade of orange
served in thin stemmed crystal
I let the liquid fill my throat and what I hoped was
hatred go down with the drink
he played with one of his diamond cuff links
while trying to enjoy the band that was playing
tonight
Well it's like this
I met you through a friend
as luck would have it
a party I cannot remember
it was right after labor day
I fell for you right there
a bell rang
my cheeks flushed
my heart soared
continued for many years
I no longer hear the bell
my cheeks still flush but with anger disappointment
it is full of grief now
I had to break my own heart

too many times
to love you
for us to work
where there is constant heartbreak
there can be no love

Like a spirit

We talk
Frequently
We meet
In secrecy
We love
Like spirits
I cannot get close to you
I cannot touch you like I want to
But I feel your presence.
Everywhere I go
In everything I do

Words

I use up a lot of them,
I use them to sometimes tell the truth.
Other times a candy-coated lie.
To sooth and to comfort
others and I
My words are mostly about thoughts and feelings.
Pain and desire
the words come to me very easily.
Faster than I can actually write them down on paper.
Interrupted
Untangled and free
From lies and deceit
Illusions and broken promises
I write as much as possible,
But now I know why.
It was to escape the jail I put myself in
from a noticeably young age
the one in my mind
a small dimly lit place
for one
With not much color

Or space
each block is built from harsh criticism.
Public reprimanding
unnecessary shame and guilt
the fear of failure
the failure to sit still like the others.
Hang on to every word my parents spoke to me.

I was not like that at all.
I followed my own rules.
Made them and broke them.
I was curious about everything.
I questioned everyone I knew.
This was always looked down upon
always chastised.
A girl had no business questioning everything that came her way.
She was expected to follow orders.
Stay in her place.
Please others
Bend over backwards for approval.
I was never able to sit still.
So, I got in trouble.
Always
not much was ever in my favor.
I was told it was because I did not listen.
Did not follow the rules.
Should not think for myself until I was able to handle that.
Handle what?
My own thoughts?
They are a mess.
A mess of insecurities
from everyone else's mistakes
But I was never allowed to speak up.
Talking back was a form of disrespect.
Even if I knew that the person speaking was wrong.
That was all a long time ago.
I do not speak up much these days.
I keep my thoughts to myself.
Words lose their value.

When they are spoken too often
the same way I might also become invaluable to some.
I write about all that I never received in the past.
I write about the things I will never have now.
I cannot live for myself.
So, I live vicariously through the characters.
They face problems.
They solve challenges.
They come to conclusions.
They find happiness.

Happiness

Happiness comes from within
I've heard this one to many times
What if all that happiness is buried
Deep
Under
Anxiety
Depression
Anger
Sarcasm
What do I do then?

Like A flower

I feel like a flower
one that is dying
one that still has all its petals
its form
but gives off no fragrance
to the world

In love with the dead

I am in love with a dead man
I have been for quite some time
A man who is no longer in my life
he lives in my mind
laughs and smiles
he haunts my dreams without any warning
I in return love him like a woman without much of a soul
a zest for life
everything is wilting
withering away
My eyes want to see him
my hands ache to hold him close
my ears miss his voice
smiles and laughter are a thing of the past
I continue to love him
despite all the distance between us
love has always been there
it has just taken a new form
It will always be there
in this life and the next
I am just damned to feel incomplete
a staggering sense of unease
for the rest of my days
which are long and unending

Time Apart

I think we need a break.
From each other
Just for a little awhile
From the stress
From your drinking
From your toxic friends
My overbearing mother
My blind father
I need you in my life.
Despite it all.
I think you need to ask yourself the same.
Am I someone you really need?

Heartache

I can never brace myself when this happens.
An air of malaise settles in
it moves around and it hovers.
Luckily never close enough to suffocate me.
Tears dangle from my lashes
Threatening to spill down my cheeks
no sound comes out
My heart sinks
All the way down to my stomach
Something falls
Something breaks
It shatters
Then it begins
The pain is debilitating.
It spreads all over
I try to process what is happening
But I can't
All there is left to do now
is somehow get out of bed

Just my 2 cents

I never had any high expectations for this relationship.
I can't love you now even if I tried.
I moved away from love so long ago.
Promised myself that I would never go looking for it again.
That I would do just fine without it
most days that's true.
I have become a stranger to love.
But then there are days when I miss having someone.
Sharing a laugh
planning the future
being held
being told that I am loved.
That I am special
I have none of that now.
I can't even begin to explain
what's missing between us.
What you don't know.
About all the things that I need
I have tried.
Multiple times
have failed.
Have been laughed at
Have been scolded,
Told that it's all fictitious.

I have nothing now.
It is amazing how the little things end up becoming the big things.
That ruin two people

Going out tonight

I am exhausted from trying to make my eyes smile.
By applying coat after coat of mascara and white eyeliner
I am exhausted from trying to make my lips smile.
By applying red lipstick and making the perfect cupid's arrow
my body screams for freedom from wearing expensive corsets all day long.
There is not much I can do.
I enjoy food and the tall glasses of colorful liquor.
It gives me comfort.
It brings me peace.
After a bad day
a terrible quarrel
Soul crushing rejection
never ending self doubt
But do not worry.
I can walk in a straight line.
Hail a cab.
Make it back to my apartment.
But sometimes I leave the keys outside.
Fall sleep with my heels on
Belly full of secrets
Head full of ideas
the exhaustion however
Never leaves me

Not the Right One

I don't think there is an easy way to say this.
But I will say it anyway.
I don't think I am right for you.
Quite frankly I don't think I ever was.
When I think about all the times, I got you in trouble
even though I had always wanted to do the right
thing.
When I think about all the times, I made you cry
Even if my only intention had been to get you to
smile.
I remember all the times we were happy.
But I had to go ruin things by saying the wrong thing.
Once again it was an attempt to make you smile.
But you frowned for the rest of the day.
There was nothing I could do to erase that.
I know you will disagree with me if you ever read this.
You handled everything so lovingly.
But I could not see that.
I was always a moment too late.
You accepted me with open arms and asked no
further questions.
You fought for me with those closest to you.
I was just aware of this.
I could not understand why you looked so upset on

some days.
I always thought I did something wrong.
But I guess it's hard to stay happy when everyone you
meet is telling you that your wrong
That you deserve so much better
So, it's time for me to leave now.
I only hope my departure brings you peace.

Some Things Never Change

The days have stretched into years
7 years to be exact
The old hair is gone
I am no longer afraid of makeup
I finally have curves
A personality to match as well
I can smile with ease
I can laugh with heart
I remind myself
To never visit the past
To never let myself experience all the things that had been ugly and distorted between us
I remind myself to never become victim of unfair treatment
I now pride myself in being able to not cry in front of others
Or in private
So I guess what I am trying to say
Is that I have made it
I have finally become the woman I wanted to be
7 years later
But then something still torments me
I feel shame
The shame that comes from missing you
From wanting to lose myself in your arms
To forget the rest of the world

From wanting to be kissed by you
to feel alive again

Normalcy

Why can't I smile?
Knowing that you're finally happy
Far away from me
with someone else
I don't think I've forgotten how to smile.
It is just that my lips can't form one.
At your memory
instead something aches inside of me
it sometimes breaks.
It sometimes bleeds.
There is a catch my in my throat.
The closest I ever get to are tears.

Years Later

I agreed to meet him.
We had been friends.
Most agreed that this was all a big fluke.
We shared a few memories.
Only to later drift apart
promised to keep in touch.
But that never happened.
Life kept us apart.
I stopped thinking about him.
After some time
But I wouldn't say that I had completely forgotten him.
I agreed to meet him.
On a sunny morning
in a bright red dress
Heels too
I was simply walking along.
When I saw someone like him in the distance
I walked closer.
Out of curiosity
it was him after all.
Just older
Sober
Looking serious

He was waiting for the bus
Wearing jeans and a leather jacket
Looking not at all bothered about anything
A cigarette in his hands
Shades in his dark hair
Eyes fixed on something.
Or someone
I checked to see if there was anyone behind me.
There was no one.
His smile got bigger.
My heart smiled.
Just a little bit
He was fixated by me.

Ice cream Sundae

I made a promise to myself.
Not too long ago
to find something to be grateful for
something to be happy about.
Every single day
So far, I think I am doing alright
to be happy for more than a day at a time
It was a new experience.
It felt scary too.
I was not able to fully enjoy this feeling.
I was afraid of it suddenly going away.
It was almost like being presented a big chocolate fudge ice cream sundae.
Then being asked to eat it with the smallest spoon.
Impossible to finish in one setting.
Did not want to waste it either.
The first few bites are pleasant.
But then everything after that feels forced
Painful to swallow
the same way I am afraid that my happiness will soon run out.
Won't come back until much later.

365

What a year
I hope to never have another one like it
I lost parts of my old self through luck, trial and error
then the great depression started and wouldn't go away
it stayed with me as I tried to move forward
As I tried to move past the heavy winds of negativity
and chaos that resided in my mind for years
It was impossible to do some days
since I had to do everything on my own
I will admit that I am not responsible for all of my mistakes
some of them are the result of other people's doing,
and flawed ideologies
I had to smile and go through the motions every single day
when all I wanted was to walk down an empty dark abyss
hoped that one day something would swallow me whole and nothing would remain
all my bad memories would be erased
my ending would not be remembered nor mourned
But that was not going to happen
in a roomful of people I still felt alone
unappreciated and disrespected
I screamed and yelled to be heard
but my voice was nothing more than a whisper to the people

to those who claimed to be family
who pride themselves in being nice and caring
but I knew they failed me a long time ago
so I decided once and for all that I would keep to myself
focus on myself and no one else
this was hard to do with a faulty memory and frail
brain that has turned to mush in some ways because
of long term beatings and bashings from years ago by
so called friends, fickle family and a two cent society
It took over 356 days for me to wipe away most of
the marks and scars that were felt behind from
childhood
take my heart off my sleeve and protect it at all times
break down the walls of terror and pain
smile when I thought it was appropriate
and never let anyone know what I set out to do next
I no longer thought it was necessary to do so much
for others
I have given to much of myself to the ungrateful
now I think twice
but I still know when to be kind, gentle and patient
I am slowly becoming the type of person I needed
when I was young, lost and misguided
the type that holds hands, and never strays too far
disciplines with love and not just ancient rules and
regulations set by dead old men or miserable hags.
I can finally admit to myself that I am feeling better
now
I did not give in to my own misery
I did not become comfortable with my own sadness
and let it rule me
I moved forward to do better

To find the appropriate ending to this horrible
chapter of my life
I feel a million pounds lighter
I smile because I want to
it is never for show now
I talk only when I have to
I understand that I matter too
I have finally learned to put myself first
I am finally happy on my own

About the Author

Farzana Habib

Farzana Habib is 29, a Scorpio and a full-time bookie. She has been writing since the age of 12 and is currently working on a horror/thriller based book called The Woman in the Painting. She loves cooking, travelling, watching movies and reading comics in her spare time.

www.ingramcontent.com/pod-product-compliance
Lightning Source LLC
La Vergne TN
LVHW041635070526
838199LV00052B/3379

9789362695956